The
BIG Purple
Book of
Beginner
Books

The BIG Purple Book of

Beginner Books

By Helen Palmer and P. D. Eastman,
Roy McKie and P. D. Eastman,
Michael Frith and P. D. Eastman,
P. D. Eastman, and Peter Eastman

RANDOM HOUSE
NEW YORK

Visit us on the Web!
randomhouse.com/kids

Educators and librarians, for a variety of teaching tools, visit us at
randomhouse.com/teachers

ISBN: 978-0-307-97587-4
Library of Congress Control Number: 2012933580

Printed in the United States of America

20

First Edition

Contents

A Fish Out Of Water

By Helen Palmer

Illustrated by P. D. Eastman

"This little fish,"
I said to Mr. Carp,
"I want him.
I like him.
And he likes me.
I will call him Otto."

"Very well," said Mr. Carp.
"Now I will tell you
how to feed him."

Then Mr. Carp told me:
"When you feed a fish,
never feed him a lot.
So much and no more!
Never more than a spot,
or something may happen!
You never know what."

Then I took Otto home.

I gave him some food.

I did not give him much.

Just one little spot!

But this did not make Otto happy.

He wanted more food.

He had to have more.

Poor Otto!

He just HAD to have more!

I knew what Mr. Carp
had told me:
   "Never feed him a lot.
   Never more than a spot!
   Or something may happen.
   You never know what."
But I gave Otto all the food
in the box.

Then something DID happen.

My little Otto began to grow.

I saw him grow.

I saw him grow and grow.

Soon he was too big

for his little fish bowl.

There was just one thing to do.

I put Otto into the flower bowl.

"There, Otto," I said.

"This will hold you."

But, no!

The flower bowl did not hold him.

Otto went right on growing!

This was not funny.

Not funny at all!

His tail was growing

right out of the top.

I grabbed the flower bowl.

I ran with it.

"Otto," I said,

"I know just where to put you.

Then you will be all right."

I put him in a big pot.

But Otto was not all right.

I saw him grow some more.

Very soon he was too big

for the pot.

I put him in pot after pot.

He was growing so fast.

Poor Otto!

My poor little fish!

Oh, why did I feed him so much?

"Otto," I said,

"stop growing! Please!"

But Otto could not stop growing.

He was growing all the time.

Very soon I ran out of pots.

Otto had to have water.

There was just one thing to do.

I did it.

I grabbed him.

I grabbed him by the tail.

I ran with him.

Up to the tub!

The tub is big.

It can hold lots of water.

At last!

"There, Otto," I said.

"This tub holds my father.

This tub holds my mother.

So, it will hold you."

But the tub did not
hold him at all.
He went right on growing.
"Oh, Otto," I said,
"what can I do now?"

Then—crash!
The door went down.
Crash!
Otto went down.
I went down, too.
Oh, what a ride!

Down went the water
into the cellar.
And down went Otto, too.
I had to do something fast.
I grabbed the phone.

I called a policeman.

"Help! Help!" I said.

"I fed my fish too much.

Mr. Carp told me not to.

But I did!"

"What?" said the policeman.
"Mr. Carp told you not to
but you did? Too bad!
I will come at once."

The policeman came.

"My fish went that way," I said.

"He is down in the cellar."

The policeman ran down with me.

"What a fish!" he said.

"He is much too big to
keep in a cellar.
We will have to get him out."

We had to work and work
to get Otto out.
Poor Otto!
Oh, why did I feed him too much?
Mr. Carp told me
something would happen.
And it did. It did!

Now we had Otto out of the cellar.

But now Otto had no water.

No water at all!

"A fish has to have water,"
I said to the policeman.
"We must take him to water.
Get help!
Call for help on the radio."

The policeman called on the radio.

He called for the firemen.

"Help! Help!" he said.

"A boy has fed a fish too much!"

"A boy has fed a fish too much?

We will come at once."

The firemen came.

They all helped to get Otto up.

"But where can we take him?"

I asked. "Up town? Down town?"

"To the pool!"

yelled the firemen.

"To the pool!"

I yelled.

"And please hurry!"

They did hurry.

The fire truck with Otto

came right up to the pool.

The firemen yelled,

"Every one get out of the pool!

This fish is going in."

Down into the pool went Otto.

Into the pool

with a big, big splash!

Now I was happy.

Now, at last, my Otto had water.

Lots of water!

This big pool was just the thing.

This big pool would hold him.

But Otto went right on growing.
And no one wanted Otto in the pool.
They did not like Otto at all.
"You take that fish out of here!"
they yelled.

There was just one thing to do.

I did it. I ran to the phone.

I called Mr. Carp.

"Please, please help me!" I said.

"I fed Otto too much."

"Oh, dear!" said Mr. Carp.

"So you fed him too much!

I knew you would.

I always say 'don't'

but you boys always do.

Yes, I will come."

Then Mr. Carp came.

He had a black box in his hand.

He had a lot of other things, too.

"What are you going to do, Mr. Carp?"
I asked him.

But Mr. Carp said nothing.

He just went right up to the pool.

He took his black box with him
and all the other things, too.
SPLASH!
Mr. Carp jumped into the pool.

SPLASH!

Now Otto went down, too!

All I could see was his tail.

I could not see Mr. Carp at all.

What was going on down there?

What were they doing down

there in the water?

Now I could see nothing.

Not Otto.

Not Mr. Carp.

Nothing at all.

Would I see my Otto again?

Would I see Mr. Carp again?

"Mr. Carp, Mr. Carp!"
I yelled. "What are you doing?
Are you all right?"

Then up jumped Mr. Carp.

In his hand was a little fish bowl.

In the bowl was my Otto!

Mr. Carp had made him little again.

"Don't ask me how I did it," he said.

"But here is your fish."

"And from now on," said Mr. Carp,
"PLEASE don't feed him too much.
Just so much, and no more!"

Now that is what I always do.
Now I feed Otto
so much and no more.
Never more than a spot
or something may happen.

And now I know what!

Snow

Roy McKie and P. D. Eastman

Snow!

Snow! Snow!

Come out in the snow.

Snow! Snow!

Just look at the snow!

Come out! Come out!

Come out in the snow.

I want to know

If you like snow.

Do you like it?

Yes or no?

Oh yes! Oh yes!

I do like snow.

Do you like it

In your face?

Yes!

I like it any place.

What is snow?

We do not know.

But snow is lots of fun,

We know.

What makes it snow?

We do not know.

But snow is fun

To dig and throw.

Snow is good

For me and you,

For men and women,

Horses, too.

Snow is good.

It makes you slide.

It lets you give

Your dog a ride.

Snow is good

For making tracks . . .

And making pictures
With your backs.

We go up hill.

The snow is deep.

We can't go fast.

The hill is steep.

We think our dog

Has gone to sleep.

But then we get

Up top at last.

Then down we come.

We come down fast!

Sometimes we put on

Long, long feet

And walk up

Every hill we meet.

Down hill we fly!
Down hill we sail!
Our dog sails after,
On his tail.

What a silly
Thing to do!
Are your feet
Too long for you?

Come on! Get up!

Get on your way!

We have a lot

To do today.

Now take some snow
And make a ball.

A lot of snow balls

Make a wall.

Put on more snow balls

One by one.

Our house of snow

Will soon be done.

Do you like bread?

Do you like meat?

Come in our house.

Come in and eat.

Snow is lots of fun,

All right!

It gives you

A big appetite.

We had our bread.

We had our meat.

Some bread is left

For birds to eat.

115

Now make another

Ball of snow.

Push it! Push it!

See it go.

What a snow ball!

See it grow!

See it grow

And grow and grow!

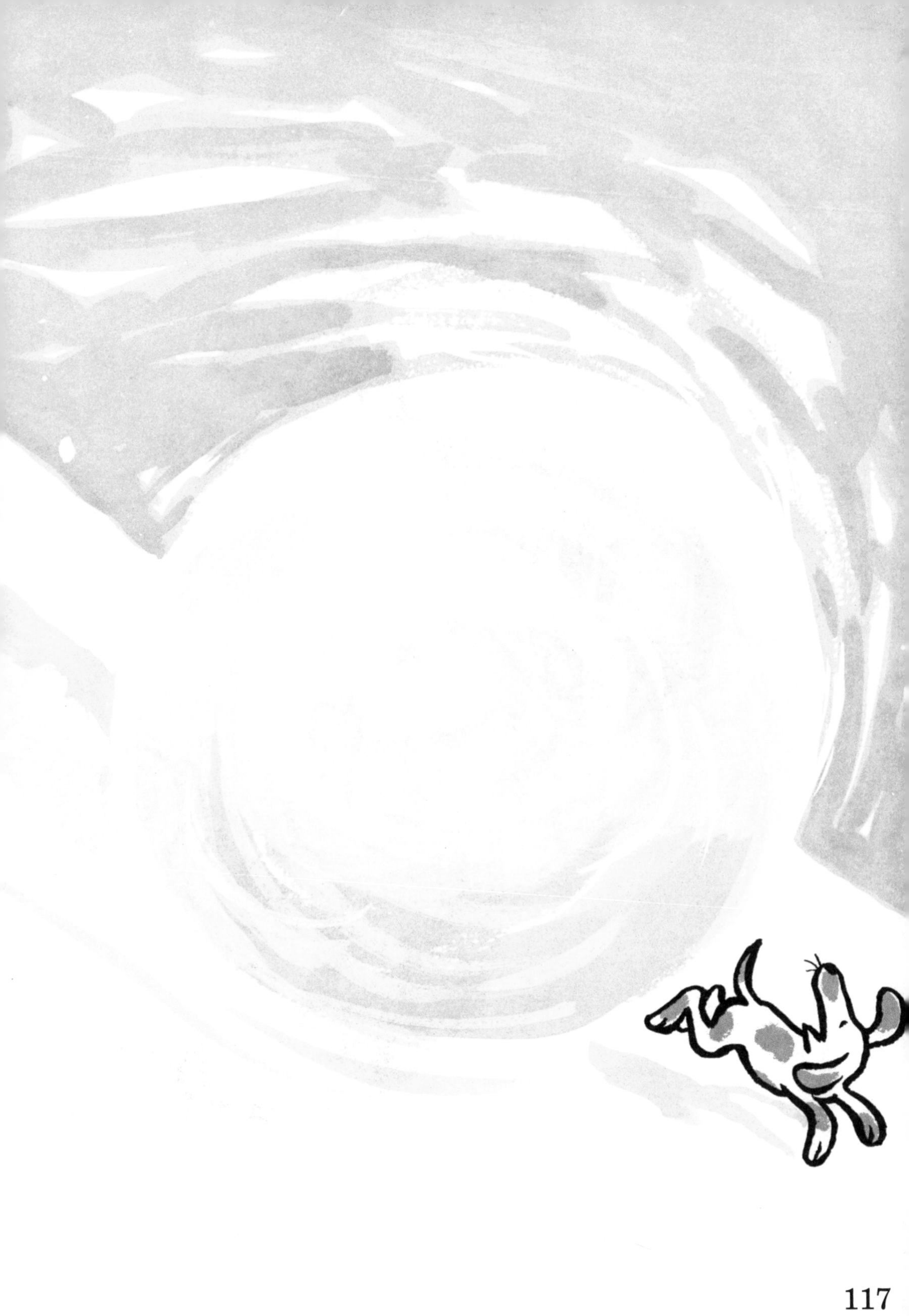

What will we make?

Let's make a man!

Let's make the biggest

Man we can!

We will call

Our snow man Ned.

But first

He has to have a head.

His head will have

To have a hat.

His hat is on.

Just look at that!

He is so big.

He is so tall.

He is the biggest

Man of all!

The sun! That sun!

It came out fast.

Do you think Ned

Is going to last?

Keep that sun
Away from Ned!
That sun is going
To his head.

The biggest snow man

Of them all

Is very, very,

Very small.

The way that sun

Is coming down,

There soon will be

No snow in town!

Take some! Save it

From the sun!

Take all you can

And run! Run! Run!

The snow out there
Will come and go,
But snow will keep
In here, we know.

So we will put
This snow away
And play with it
Some other day.

I'll Teach My Dog 100 Words

by Michael Frith

Illustrated by

P. D. Eastman

I'll teach my dog 100 words.

The first six words
I'll teach my pup
are . . .

dig a hole!

And

fill it up!

I'll teach him . . .
walk

and run,

and then . . .

catch a ball!

Now that makes ten.

And Mr. Smith,
who lives next door,
will say, "That's great!
Can you
teach him more?"

And then I'll teach him . . .

bark

and
beg

and
wag your tail

and
shake a leg . . .

and
wash your ears

and
wash your toes!

and
scratch your head
and
blow your nose!

Then Mr. Smith
will tell
Miss Brown,
"This is
the smartest
dog in town!"

143

I won't stop there.
No, not at all . . .

I'll teach him big,

I'll teach him small . . .

and fat and thin

and short and tall . . .

and dark . . .

and light . . .

146

and day . . .

and night.

And then
Miss Brown
will call
Miss May.
"Come over
right away,"
she'll say.

"This dog
is learning
chase the cat
and
climb the tree
and
things like that!"

Then we will give them more
to see . . .

eat your food

and follow me.

Wow!
We're up to
forty-three.

I'll teach him

RED and BLUE and GREEN

"The smartest dog we've ever seen!"

I'll teach him

That makes forty-nine, I think.

And then Miss May
will call Mayor Meer.
She'll call,
"Please
hurry
over here!"

And then for Mr. Meer,
the Mayor,
I'll teach my dog . . .
now paint the chair!

Paint the road from here
to there.

HERE

Then Mr. Meer, the Mayor, will say,
"I'll make today a holiday!"

And everyone will come to see
my amazing dog and me.

We'll show   and
them skate   kick the stone!

Jump the fishbowl!

Bring
the bone!

Chew the boot,
and hold the phone!

Cut the grass!

Shine my shoe!

Comb your hair!

And clean the zoo!

Now
brush the bear!

That's
eighty-two.

But that's not all my dog will do.

He'll tickle the pig,

and kiss the goose!

He'll feed the mouse,

and mop the moose!

He'll
toot a bugle . . .

beat a drum.

He'll stand on
Uncle Abner's thumb.

And then
I'll teach him
sing with
the birds.

Now, THERE!
That makes
100 words.

My dog will learn
those hundred words—
and how my friends will cheer!

I'll teach my dog
those hundred words . . .

. . . I think I'll start next year.

Flap Your Wings

by P. D. Eastman

An egg lay in the path.

A boy came down the path.

He saw the egg.

He looked around.

He saw flamingos and frogs,

and turtles and alligators.

"Whose egg is this?" he called.

But nobody answered.

Then the boy looked up.

He saw an empty nest in a tree.

"Here is an egg without a nest," he said,

"and there is a nest without an egg."

The boy climbed the tree.

He put the egg

in the nest.

Then he went away.

Mr. and Mrs. Bird came home.

They were surprised to find

an egg in their nest.

"That's not **our** egg," said Mrs. Bird.

"Look how big it is!"

"But it is an egg. It's in our nest,"
said Mr. Bird.
"If an egg is in your nest,
you sit on it and keep it warm.
It doesn't matter
whose egg it is."

"All right," said Mrs. Bird.
"But I wonder what kind of bird
will come out of that egg."

They took turns keeping the egg warm.

First Mrs. Bird sat on it.

Then Mr. Bird sat on it.

And sometimes,
because it was so big,
they both sat on it.

One day Mrs. Bird heard
a squeaking noise.
"Help!" she said.
"This egg is squeaking!"

Mr. Bird came back to the nest.

He listened to the egg.

"The egg is not squeaking," he said.

"It's our baby that is squeaking.

He is ready to come out of the egg."

Mr. and Mrs. Bird waited.

177

The egg started to crack.

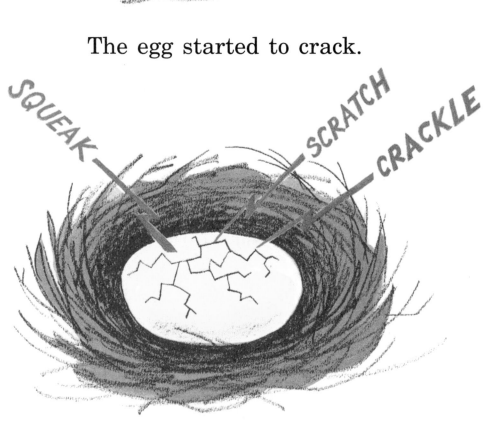

Then it cracked some more.

And there was the baby!

Mr. Bird was very excited.

"It's Junior!" he shouted.

"What a beautiful baby!"

Junior opened his mouth.

It was a big mouth.

It was full of teeth.

"That's the funniest-looking baby
I ever saw," said Mrs. Bird.

"Something is wrong.

I don't think he's our baby at all!"

"He's in our nest, so he must
be ours," said Mr. Bird.
"His mouth is open.
That means he's hungry.
When your baby is hungry,
you feed him."
Mr. and Mrs. Bird went away
to get some food for Junior.

Mr. Bird brought
a pink worm.

Mrs. Bird brought
a green one.

Junior ate both worms
in one gulp.
Then he opened
his mouth wide again.
"We have to get Junior
lots more to eat,"
said Mr. and Mrs. Bird.

Hour after hour, day after day,
they brought food for Junior.

Mrs. Bird got berries and cherries.

She got butterflies and caterpillars.

She got dragonflies and mosquitoes.

She got ladybugs and tiger beetles.

Mr. Bird got crickets and spiders.

He got grasshoppers and snails.

He got red ants.

He got black ants.

He got centipedes, too!

"What kind of bird

eats so much?" said Mrs. Bird.

"It doesn't matter," said Mr. Bird.

"He's still hungry

and we have to feed him."

Weeks went by.

Junior never stopped eating.

And he never . . .

. . . stopped growing.

He grew **bigger** . . .

and **bigger** . . .

and bigger!

Finally Junior got so big
that Mr. Bird said,
"It's too crowded up here.
Junior has to leave the nest.
It is time for him
to fly away."

"You are right," said Mrs. Bird.

"The time has come.

We must show him

how to fly."

Mrs. Bird pushed
and pushed.

Mr. Bird showed Junior how to fly.

"Jump into the air like this," he said.

"Then flap your wings."

Junior got ready.

He took a big breath

and jumped.

Up . . . up . . . up into the air

he went.

"Flap your wings!" yelled Mrs. Bird.

"Flap your wings!" yelled Mr. Bird.

Junior flapped and flapped.

But it didn't do any good.

He didn't have any wings!

Down . . . down . . . down went Junior.

Down into the water.

SPLASH!

It was cool and wet in the water.

It was just right for Junior.

"You know," said Mrs. Bird,

"I don't think Junior was a bird at all!"

"It doesn't matter," Mr. Bird said.

"He's happy now.

And just look at him swim!"

Big Dog...
Little Dog

by P. D. Eastman

Fred and Ted were friends.

Fred was big.

Ted was little.

Fred always had money.

Ted never had money.

When they walked in the rain,

Fred was wet . . .

and Ted was dry.

They both liked music.

Fred played
the flute.

Ted played
the tuba.

When they had dinner,

Fred ate the spinach . . .

and Ted ate the beets.

When they painted the house,

Fred used green paint.

Ted used red.

One day Fred and Ted
went away in their cars.

Fred went in
his green car.

FRED

TED

Ted went in
his red car.

Fred drove his car slowly.

Ted drove his car fast.

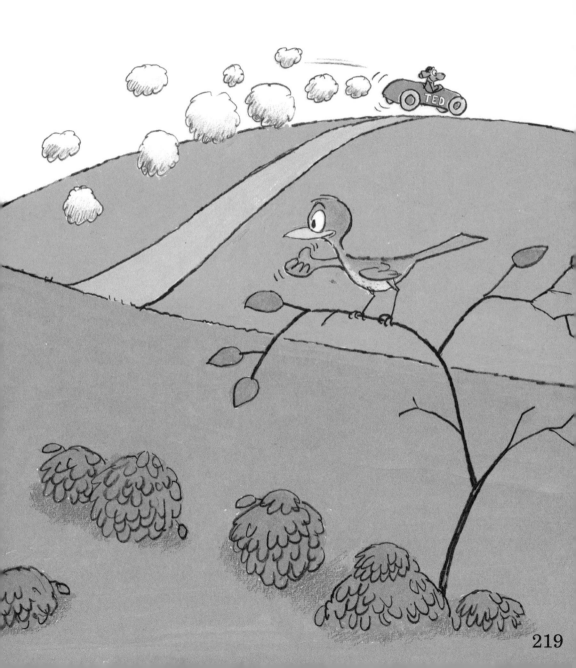

They came to a sign.

"Where should we go?" asked Fred.

"To the mountains," said Ted.

When they got to the mountains,

Ted skied all day long.

Fred skated all day long.

When they stopped,

Fred was cold.

Ted was warm.

By night both of them
were very sleepy.
"Look!" said Fred.
"A small hotel!"

Fred's room was upstairs.

Ted's room was downstairs.

"Good night, Ted.
Sleep well," said Fred.

"Good night, Fred.
Sleep well," said Ted.

But they did *not* sleep well.
Upstairs, Fred thumped and bumped
and tossed and turned.

Downstairs, Ted moaned and groaned
and crashed and thrashed all over the bed.

When morning came,
Fred called Ted.

"Let's take a walk,"
Fred said to Ted.

"We can walk
and talk," said Ted
to Fred.

231

They walked uphill.

They walked downhill.

They made tall talk.

They made small talk.

"Did you get any sleep
last night, Ted?"

"None at all, Fred!"

"My bed is too little!"

"My bed is too big!"

"What can we do about it, Ted?"

"I don't know, Fred."

"I know what to do!"
said the bird.
"Ted should sleep upstairs
and Fred should sleep
downstairs!"

"The bird's got the word."

"Back to bed!"
yelled Ted.

"Back to bed!"
yelled Fred.

"It's downstairs for me!"
yelled Fred.

"It's upstairs for me!"
yelled Ted.

Ted jumped into
the little bed upstairs.

And Fred jumped into
the big bed downstairs.

Ted slept all day long
in the cozy little bed.

And Fred slept all day long
in the cozy big bed.

241

"Well, that was easy to do.
Big dogs need big beds.
Little dogs need little beds.
Why make big problems
out of little problems?"

Fred
and Ted
Go Camping

by Peter Eastman

Fred and Ted were friends.

They liked to go camping in the woods.

One day they packed their cars.
They were going camping.

They drove to the woods.

Fred took many things.

Ted took few things.

They parked their cars
and walked into the woods.

Fred liked this spot.

Ted liked it, too.

Fred had a hard time with his tent.

Ted had an easy time with his tent.

That night,

Fred was awake.

Ted was asleep.

The next morning . . .

Ted woke up early.

Fred woke up late.

They took their boat to the lake.

Fred took the heavy end.

Ted took the light end.

They put the boat in the water.

Ted stayed dry.

Fred got wet.

They fished.

Ted used a net.

Fred used a pole.

Ted got ten little fish.

Fred got one BIG fish!

Splash!

The boat tipped over!

All the little fish
jumped out.

Fred and Ted swam away
from the big fish!

Ted swam fast.

Fred swam faster.

Ted ran fast.

Fred ran faster.

Now Ted
was hungry.

Fred was
hungrier.

271

Then they heard a little bird.

"Look up in a tree.

Look down at your feet.

And you will soon find

something to eat,"

sang the little bird.

Fred looked up.

He saw nothing.

Ted looked down.

He saw something.

Berries!

Fred looked up again.

Bonk!

Something hit Fred on his head.

A nut!

They even found some crab apples.

They went back to camp.

Ted ran with the berries.

Fred walked with the
apples and nuts.

They cooked the apples

and the nuts

in a pan

on a fire.

281

They ate it all up.

Ted ate slowly.

Fred ate quickly.

What about the berries?

They saved the berries for last.
Yum!

Beginner Books

ARE YOU MY MOTHER? by P. D. Eastman

THE BEARS' PICNIC by Stan and Jan Berenstain

THE BEARS' VACATION by Stan and Jan Berenstain

BECAUSE A LITTLE BUG WENT KA-CHOO! by Rosetta Stone

THE BELLY BOOK by Joe Harris

THE BERENSTAIN BEARS AND THE MISSING DINOSAUR BONE
by Stan and Jan Berenstain

THE BEST NEST by P. D. Eastman

BIG DOG . . . LITTLE DOG by P. D. Eastman

THE BIG HONEY HUNT by Stan and Jan Berenstain

THE BIKE LESSON by Stan and Jan Berenstain

CAN YOU TELL ME HOW TO GET TO SESAME STREET?
by Eleanor Hudson

THE CAT IN THE HAT by Dr. Seuss

THE CAT IN THE HAT COMES BACK by Dr. Seuss

THE CAT'S QUIZZER by Dr. Seuss

A CRACK IN THE TRACK by the Rev. W. Awdry

THE DIGGING-EST DOG by Al Perkins

DR. SEUSS'S ABC by Dr. Seuss

A FISH OUT OF WATER by Helen Palmer

FLAP YOUR WINGS by P. D. Eastman

A FLY WENT BY by Mike McClintock

FOX IN SOCKS by Dr. Seuss

FRED AND TED GO CAMPING by Peter Eastman

FRED AND TED LIKE TO FLY by Peter Eastman

FRED AND TED'S ROAD TRIP by Peter Eastman

GO, DOG. GO! by P. D. Eastman